JUSTINE McKEEN
and the BIRD NERD

JUSTINE McKEEN
and the BIRD NERD

Sigmund Brouwer
illustrated by **Dave Whamond**

ORCA BOOK PUBLISHERS

Library and Archives Canada Cataloguing in Publication

Brouwer, Sigmund, 1959-, author
Justine McKeen and the bird nerd / Sigmund Brouwer ;
illustrated by Dave Whamond.
(Orca echoes)

Issued in print and electronic formats.
ISBN 978-1-4598-0394-7 (pbk.).--ISBN 978-1-4598-0395-4 (pdf).
ISBN 978-1-4598-0396-1 (epub)

I. Whamond, Dave, illustrator II. Title. III. Series: Orca echoes
PS8553.R6846J1872 2013   jC813'.54   C2013-902330-5
                    C2013-902331-3

First published in the United States, 2013
Library of Congress Control Number: 2013937057

Summary: With the help of Justine, Jimmy Blatzo sets out to protect birds
from flying into the windows at school and the town hall.

Orca Book Publishers gratefully acknowledges the support for its publishing programs
provided by the following agencies: the Government of Canada through the Canada Book
Fund and the Canada Council for the Arts, and the Province of British Columbia
through the BC Arts Council and the Book Publishing Tax Credit.

MIX
Paper from
responsible sources
FSC® C004071

ANCIENT FOREST ™
FRIENDLY

*Orca Book Publishers is dedicated to preserving the environment and has printed
this book on Forest Stewardship Council® certified paper.*

Cover artwork and interior illustrations by Dave Whamond
Author photo by Reba Baskett

ORCA BOOK PUBLISHERS
PO Box 5626, Stn. B
Victoria, BC Canada
v8R 6s4

ORCA BOOK PUBLISHERS
PO Box 468
Custer, WA USA
98240-0468

www.orcabook.com
Printed and bound in Canada.

16 15 14 13 • 4 3 2 1

To Samantha and Jayse, with much love—you are wonderful sunshine for all of us!

Chapter One

"Yesterday after school was so embarrassing," Justine said. "The woman shouted *pig pee* at me! *Pig pee, pig pee*, she yelled. And then she slammed her door in my face."

As usual at recess, Justine was hanging out at the school flagpole with her friends Michael and Safdar and Jimmy Blatzo.

"Pig pee?" Blatzo asked.

"I know," Justine said. "Can you believe it? I had carefully explained it was pig urine. And I'm just trying to help the environment and make a little money with door-to-door sales. I guess sometimes you have to put up with stuff like that when you're the Queen of Green."

1

"Pig pee," Blatzo said. He was frowning as he thought about it.

"Think that's embarrassing?" Safdar said to Justine. "On Saturday, I was walking through the park with some friends and I had to yawn."

"What's so embarrassing about that?" Michael asked.

"I yawned while I was walking through a spider web," Safdar answered. "And the spider *and* the fly that it was eating went right into my mouth. Even worse, I accidentally chewed before I could spit it out!"

"Pig pee," Blatzo said again. His frown grew deeper.

"Pig urine," Justine told Blatzo. "Get over it."

"Oh yeah?" Michael said. "Let me tell you about embarrassing. Yesterday at supper, I jokingly told my dad that his boss had called and said he was fired. But my dad took it seriously and phoned his boss and called him a bunch of names. Then my dad really did get fired from his job!"

Justine looked at Michael. "That's horrible. Your dad got fired?"

"No," Michael said. "I just thought if you guys were making up embarrassing stories, I would too."

"Hang on," Safdar said. "I really did eat a spider. It was disgusting."

"And I wasn't making mine up either," Justine said. "People get just plain silly when you try to sell them plastic disposable plates made with pig urine."

"Permission to speak to you?" Safdar asked Blatzo.

Blatzo nodded. Blatzo was big and liked to threaten Michael and Safdar.

"Do you have any embarrassing stories?" Safdar asked.

"Not anything about pig pee or chewing spiders," Blatzo said. "But I did cry once over a dead bird. It was so cute and tiny, and it flew right into that window over there."

Blatzo pointed at one of the front windows of the school. "I saw it hit the glass and fall. When I got there, it was gasping for air. I held it in my hands and it died. I couldn't help it. I started crying."

"Maybe if it had happened yesterday, that would be embarrassing," Michael said. "Everybody knows how tough you are. But you were probably in kindergarten, right? Everybody cries in kindergarten."

"No," Blatzo said. "I wasn't in kindergarten." Tears began to roll down his face, and he rubbed his eyes. "It happened yesterday."

Justine put an arm on Blatzo's shoulder.

Michael and Safdar were smart enough not to say a word. Especially without permission from Jimmy Blatzo.

Chapter Two

At lunch hour the next day, Justine saw Mr. Noble, the school janitor, at the end of the hallway. There were plenty of students in the hallway to hide behind. She began to sneak up on him.

It didn't work. Mr. Noble noticed her and began to run. Well, it wasn't a run. Nobody was supposed to run in the hallways at school. It was a really fast walk that looked like a run.

He made it around the corner before Justine could get there. It didn't matter though. Justine went straight to the janitor's workroom. The door was locked.

"Ha," Justine said. "Got you."

She knocked on the door.

No answer.

"Mr. Noble," she said. "It's me. Justine. You've locked the door again."

"Go away," he said from the other side of the door. "Stop chasing me. I don't want to talk to you about pig pee. I don't want to talk to *anyone* about pig pee."

"Pig urine. And if you open the door, I'll tell you who put squished worms in your sandwiches."

"You are lying just to get me to open the door." His voice was muffled.

"No," Justine said. "Take a look at your lunch."

She waited.

Five seconds later, she heard a yell inside the workroom.

The door opened. Mr. Noble's face was red. He held out an open peanut butter sandwich filled with worms. "Someone *did* put squished worms in my sandwiches! Tell me who."

"Me," Justine said. "You really should keep the door locked when you're not around. Instead of locking it to avoid innocent young girls trying to help the environment."

"Innocent!" His face stayed red. "You put squished worms in my sandwiches!"

"Of course," she said. "How else was I going to get you to open the door? But don't worry. I didn't kill the worms. I found them dead on the sidewalk after the rain."

Mr. Noble looked completely lost for words.

Justine stuck her foot out so that Mr. Noble couldn't close the door again. "Now, let's talk about you buying some plates."

"Plates made out of pig pee," he said. "Trust me, I've heard all about this from the teachers."

"Yes," Justine said. "You are last on my list. And try to think of it as pig urine." She pushed past him into his workroom.

"First," she said, "if you look in the top drawer of your workbench, you'll see where I hid some good sandwiches to make up for the worms."

"But what if you hadn't stopped me in time? I could have eaten squished worms and —"

"Second," she said, "do you want to pay with credit card, check or cash? Disposable plastic plates are made from fossil fuels and are bad for the environment. But a company in Denmark uses pig urine —"

"Pig pee!"

"Pig urine has many health hazards and costs a lot of money to dispose of. So this company turns pig urine into bioplastics. It's a win-win situation! How many plates would you like?"

Mr. Noble sighed. "I'll take two orders. As long as you promise to stop chasing me around the school at lunch hour."

"Good," she said.

"So how many orders have you sold?"

"Including yours?" she asked.

"Including mine."

"Two," Justine said. "You wouldn't believe how many people don't want plates made of pig pee."

Then Justine frowned. She saw a clear plastic bag in the corner of the workroom. Inside it were three small dead birds.

Chapter Three

"I remember one morning when I was really sick to my stomach," Safdar said. "I ran as fast as I could for the bathroom, but I wasn't going to make it. I saw a shopping bag on the kitchen table, so I threw up in the bag instead of the toilet."

Justine, Michael, Safdar and Blatzo were standing near the flagpole again at afternoon recess.

"That's not so embarrassing," Michael said. "Anyone would do that."

"Except the bag was filled with all of my mom's tax papers," Safdar said. "And she had just spent the night before getting her tax return ready."

Michael clapped. "Excellent flagpole story. True or false?"

Justine voted for true. So did Blatzo. Michael voted for false. All of them looked at Safdar.

"Sadly, true," he said. "But my dad understood. He said that taxes always make him feel like throwing up."

"Once I went into a fitting room at a department store," Blatzo said. "I closed the door and yelled as loud as I could, *Hey, where's the toilet paper?* You wouldn't believe how fast the clerks came running to tell me it wasn't a bathroom."

"True," Justine said.

"True," Michael said.

"True," Safdar said.

"False," Blatzo said.

They all laughed. Blatzo gave them a big grin.

"Last week," Michael began, "my older brother thanked my mom for leaving an extra toothbrush in the shower. He said it helped him clean between his toes."

"That sounds like a good idea," Safdar said. "I should try that."

"Not with my toothbrush!" Michael said. "That's where I had been leaving it. For two weeks."

"Wow," Justine said. "Great flagpole story. I can't decide. True or false. Blatzo?"

She expected him to tell her not to call him Blatzo. Instead, he said, "I have to go."

"In a bathroom, not a fitting room. Right?" Michael said.

Blatzo answered by pointing at the school window, where some kindergarten kids were crouched in a circle. Then Blatzo ran to the front doors of the school and went inside.

Justine, Michael and Safdar walked over to see what the little kids were doing.

They saw a small brown bird with a white speckled breast lying on the ground in the middle of the circle.

"It flew into the window," one of the little girls said. She started to sob. "I don't want it to die."

Justine knelt beside the bird. It was blinking its eyes. It was sad to see the poor bird suffering.

Now she thought she understood why Blatzo had run away. He didn't want to cry again.

Chapter Four

"What do we do?" Safdar asked. "How do you give first aid to a bird?"

"You move over," a voice said behind them.

It was Blatzo. He was holding a cardboard shoe box.

"I got this from the office," he said. "Give me some room."

Blatzo handed the box and a pen to Justine. "Poke some holes in the top, okay? If the bird lives, it's going to need air."

Justine saw that a paper towel had been folded and placed on the bottom of the box. As she poked holes in the box with the pen, Blatzo got on his knees and looked closely at the bird. "We all need

to be as quiet as possible. Birds can die from fright. Especially tiny birds like this one."

Blatzo didn't touch the bird. There were tears in his eyes. "At least we don't see any blood. And it isn't gasping for air."

His voice was soft as he kept speaking. "You are also supposed to look for swelling around the eyes or head. I don't see that either. It wouldn't be good if one eye was open and the other closed. Or if one leg was curled up and the other straight. Anything lopsided would mean the bird was in real trouble."

"How do you know this?" Michael whispered.

"I just started a science project and learned about this on the Internet," Blatzo said. "Justine, can you hand me the box? Make sure the lid is off."

Justine knelt beside Blatzo. Blatzo reached into his back pocket and pulled out another piece of paper towel. He placed the paper towel completely over the bird.

"It's better if the bird's eyes are covered," he said. "It won't be as frightened when I pick it up."

Very gently, Blatzo lifted the small bird and put it in the box. He set the box on the ground and put the lid on.

"What now?" Safdar asked.

"If it was injured badly, we would take it to a vet. Our town isn't big enough to have an animal rescue shelter. But since the bird doesn't look like it's hurt too badly, we can keep it in a quiet place until after school."

Blatzo was still on his knees.

"Thank you, thank you," the little girl said. She wiped her nose clear of tears. Then she put her arms around Blatzo's neck, smearing his face with her sticky hands.

Blatzo didn't get mad at her. He didn't stand either. He let the girl hug him.

"You don't need to thank me," he said. "I know exactly how you feel."

Chapter Five

After school, Justine met Blatzo at the flagpole. He was carrying the shoe box. They began to walk to the town park, just the two of them.

"How is the bird?" Justine asked.

"I haven't looked," Blatzo said. "You're supposed to give it as much rest and quiet as possible. I was afraid that if I opened the box too soon, it would frighten the bird if it was still recovering. And if it was okay, I was afraid it might fly out of the box into the school and get hurt again."

"We could open the lid now," Justine said. "If it's ready to fly, this would be a great time."

The sky above them was clear blue. There was no wind, and it was warm. A perfect day for little birds to go free.

"Not near the school," Blatzo said. "What if it flies into a window again?"

"I should have thought of that," Justine said. "Especially after what I saw at lunch hour in Mr. Noble's workroom."

"Dead birds in a plastic bag, right?" Blatzo said.

"How did you know?"

"I saw them this morning. My teacher let me talk to Mr. Noble for my science project. I asked him if he finds dead birds outside the school window. He said he always takes them away because it makes students upset to find them."

"Like the little girl today who was crying," Justine said.

"Are you teasing me?"

"No, I meant the little girl in kindergarten. I would never tease you about crying."

Blatzo was quiet for a while as they kept walking toward the park.

"It's okay," Justine said. "That you cried."

Blatzo stayed quiet.

She waited a bit longer. Then she said, "Michael and Safdar think it's okay too."

"You guys talked about my crying?"

"No," Justine said. "A person can know things without talking about them."

"Oh," he said.

"For example, I don't ever talk to Michael and Safdar about how they try to make you happy by pretending that you scare them."

"I don't scare them?" Blatzo asked.

"Not anymore," Justine said. "It doesn't take long for people to realize that you are harmless. Have you ever really hurt anybody?"

"No," he said.

"Because you actually care about others. I knew that the first day I met you. I think you try to frighten people away because you're afraid they might not like you for who you are."

"And I think maybe I don't want to talk about this," Blatzo said.

"Okay," Justine said. "So maybe after the park, we could go to a department store and yell for toilet paper in the fitting room?"

"Only if our bird flies away," Blatzo said. "Otherwise, I'll be too sad to joke around."

Chapter Six

Justine and Blatzo reached the park and sat on the bench.

"I'm afraid to open the box," Blatzo said. He kept the box on his lap with the lid closed. "What if the bird didn't make it?"

"That would be really sad," Justine said. "Flying into a window would be like having an invisible person walk up to you and knock you in the head with an invisible bat."

"This one is a wood thrush," Blatzo said. "Just like the one I found a couple of days ago. They migrate at night. It was really cool to learn about. They use stars and the magnetic field of the Earth to find their way.

After surviving an amazing two-thousand-mile journey, something as ordinary as a window might have killed it. That's not cool."

He leaned forward, protecting the box. "I think it's great that people worry about preserving habitats to save birds, but hitting windows kills nearly as many birds as loss of habitat. I'm putting it into a report for my science project, but you don't even want to know the number."

"Tell me," Justine said.

"A billion birds every year," Blatzo said. "And unlike death by natural causes, colliding with windows takes some of the healthiest birds. Worse, many of them are songbirds like this thrush, and their populations are already dropping."

He shrugged. "I memorized that part from my science report."

"A billion birds a year!" Justine said. "Dead from hitting windows!"

"That's just a horrible number though," Blatzo answered. "Until you see one of them die right in front of you. Then it becomes real."

He held out the box. "Sometimes a bird just needs time to recover, but while it's on the ground, a cat gets it. If this one is alive, I'm glad we found it first."

"Want to wait awhile longer?" Justine asked.

"How about just a peek?" Blatzo said. He slowly lifted up one side of the lid and looked inside the box. "It's standing!"

Blatzo pulled the lid off.

Justine peeked too. The bird tilted its head and looked at her.

"Shouldn't it be flying?" she asked.

Blatzo carefully lowered his hand. He stuck out a finger and moved it toward the bird's feet. The bird's claws curled around Blatzo's finger. He lifted the bird and held it out in front of him.

For a moment, the bird stayed on his finger.

Then it fluttered upward to the big blue sky.

"Wow," Blatzo said. "That was amazing!"

"It's like it wasn't even scared of someone as big as you," Justine said. "Strange, huh?"

"We're not talking about that, okay? Besides, I want you to think about something else."

"Like what?"

"You're the Queen of Green," Blatzo said. "Selling pig-pee plates might be good for helping the world, but how about coming up with something to help the birds in our own backyard?"

Chapter Seven

Justine and Blatzo sat in the back row of a large room at the town hall. Except for a newspaper reporter, they were the only ones in the room. There was a big box on the floor at their feet.

After a few minutes, four women and three men walked into the room and took their places behind a long table at the front of the room. There was a microphone in front of each of them.

Justine pointed out Mayor Samantha Singh to Blatzo. She sat in the center. Then Justine named all the other council members for him.

"I can see their names on the signs on the table in front of them," Blatzo said. "And I learned to read a long time ago."

"Sorry," Justine whispered. "I'm a little nervous."

"I'm nervous too," Blatzo whispered back. "I never speak in public."

"My grammy said if you speak in public and are nervous, just pretend the people in the audience are wearing clown outfits," Justine whispered.

Blatzo laughed. But it was a nervous laugh.

Mayor Singh spoke. "I call this meeting to order. Let's start with the first item on our agenda. The proposed new bylaw for increasing the size of bus-stop signs."

Justine stood and raised her hand.

"Yes?" Mayor Singh said.

"Normally I wouldn't interrupt," Justine said. "But it's a school night, and my friend and I would like to speak to town council. Would it be okay if we spoke now? We both have lots of homework to do."

"I think it's wonderful when students want to participate in democracy," Mayor Singh said. She asked her council members, "All in favor?"

All of them raised their hands.

"Go ahead," Mayor Singh told Justine.

"Thank you," she answered. "My name is Justine McKeen and —"

"Justine McKeen, Queen of Green?" Councilor Mark Lopez said.

"Yes," she answered. "Some people call me that."

"Are you the girl going door to door trying to sell plates made of pig pee?" asked Councilor Mary Hull.

"Pig urine," Justine said. "It's a biohazard, so a company has converted pig urine into bioplastics —"

"We are not interested in pig-pee plates for the town," Councilor Hull said. Some council members laughed.

"We need to listen seriously to Justine," Mayor Singh said. "She and the kids at her school have organized some great green projects in town.

Like a greenhouse and a walking school bus. And finding a good use for wasted food."

"Don't forget the T-shirts for the Pooper Scooper campaign," Councilor Lopez said. "A lot of parents got involved with the school board because of that. Kids can make a difference."

"Thank you for pointing that out," Mayor Singh said. "We all like to keep parents happy, right Councilor Hull? Justine, what is it you want town council to consider?"

"Nothing," Justine said. "It's my friend Jimmy Blatzo who has something to show you. I might be the Queen of Green, but he's the Bird Nerd."

"Bird Nerd?" Jimmy hissed.

"I just thought of it," Justine whispered. "In politics, you need a name people will remember. Notice that the newspaper reporter just wrote that down. It will probably be in the paper tomorrow."

"Bird Nerd?" he hissed again. "In the town newspaper?"

"Stop talking to me," she said with her teeth closed in a wide smile. "Town council is waiting for you."

Blatzo stood. He tried to speak. But he was too nervous.

Finally, he picked up the box at his feet, walked to the front and presented it to Mayor Singh.

She smiled like she thought it was a present and opened it.

Then she gasped.

"What kind of sick joke is this?" she sputtered. "The box is full of dead birds!"

Chapter Eight

"It wasn't meant to be a joke," Blatzo said. "These are birds I found in front of town hall in the last week."

"What?" Mayor Singh asked. She looked closer. "There are at least thirty dead birds in this box. I never see dead birds when I get here."

"That's because when they hit the windows and die, scavenger birds like crows or gulls take them away," Blatzo answered. "Or cats and raccoons find them. Also, most of them fall into the bushes below the window and nobody sees them."

"Thirty birds?" Councilor Lopez said. "Let me see."

Mayor Singh passed the box up and down the table for all the council members to see.

"This is so sad," Councilor Hull said. "All of these birds died in one week?"

"It was hard for me," Blatzo said. "But every day for the last week, I came looking for them. I thought if I showed you instead of just telling you, you might begin to care about it as much as I do."

"Thirty dead birds in one week is a lot," Mayor Singh said.

"That's just the ones I found," Blatzo answered. "It might be fifty or sixty birds a week."

"Just from hitting our windows?" Councilor Lopez said.

"Millions of birds die all across the country every week," Blatzo said. "About a billion a year. And we really don't know about it because only once in a while do we see the dead birds."

"That's horrible," Councilor Hull said. "We need to do something so the birds stop hitting our windows at town hall. And maybe get other people in town thinking about what we can do to help."

41

"I'm glad you said that," Blatzo said. "I happen to have an idea."

"Good," Mayor Singh said. "We are here to listen."

"I hope you like it," Blatzo said. "Especially because it can make some extra money for the town."

Chapter Nine

At the flagpole, Safdar had a new story for Michael and Justine. "After school yesterday, I went into my room and found a plastic snake on the floor. My sister was in the living room, so I yelled to her that she couldn't fool me. Then I picked up the snake and it bit me! I had to go to the hospital."

"You have to do better than that," Michael said.

"Sorry," Justine said. "I agree with Michael. That's a lame flagpole story."

"Well, how about the time that I grabbed an electric fence and wet my pants?"

"You told us that one yesterday," Michael said. "We won't believe it today either."

Safdar sighed.

Blatzo hurried toward them. He grinned like he had something to tell them.

"Permission to ask why you look so happy?" Michael asked.

"Permission never to ask for permission again," Blatzo said. "I'm done with that. How about listening to what I got on my science project? One hundred percent!"

"I'm thinking false," Safdar said. "Michael?"

"False," Michael said. "And as a flagpole story, very boring."

"Maybe we need to go back to permissions again," Blatzo growled.

Michael and Safdar laughed.

"Messing with you!" Safdar said. Michael and Safdar gave Blatzo high fives.

"If you didn't get one hundred percent," Justine told Blatzo, "I would have dragged your science teacher out here to look at our beautiful new windows."

"They do look good," Blatzo said.

He admired the windows with Justine, Safdar and Michael.

Each window was covered with a giant word of inspiration, like *Dream*, *Courage* or *Kindness*.

That's because each window had a one-way film advertisement. From the inside of the classrooms, students could see out as if the windows were crystal clear. But from the outside, the giant letters were obvious. And because the windows no longer looked clear from the outside, birds had stopped flying into the glass.

"Didn't cost a penny either," Justine said.

Even though Blatzo had asked her for help, in the end it had been Blatzo's idea. They had done some research on the Internet and learned about companies that sold advertising with one-way films.

Blatzo had called the president of a nearby company and asked to make a deal. Blatzo would get the town council to sell advertising to local businesses, using one-way film on the windows at town hall.

The town would then pay the company for the film but still make a little money from the advertising. In exchange, the film company agreed to put one-way film on the school windows for free.

"And," Justine added, "if you didn't get one hundred percent on your project, I would have marched in and showed your teacher the email that the town council sent out to every household. It had some great advice on how to prevent birds from running into the windows of homes."

"One hundred percent." Blatzo smiled. "That's never happened to me before."

"And neither has this," Justine said. She whistled to get the attention of the kindergarten kids who had found the wood thrush by the window a few weeks earlier.

They came running. The little girl who had cried on Blatzo's shoulder held a bag.

She handed it to Blatzo.

"A present," the little girl said. "For you."

Chapter Ten

Blatzo pulled something out of the bag. It was a folded bright-pink T-shirt.

"That's the color for anti-bullying," Justine said.

"Like I didn't know?" Blatzo said. "This is not something we need to talk about again. I will wear it proudly."

"Good," Michael said. "That means if you get mad at what the T-shirt says, we won't have to run away."

"But if you don't like it," said Safdar, "remember that I told them it was a bad idea to make the shirt for you. And I'm going to keep my distance. Just in case it *is* something we need to talk about again."

Blatzo unfolded the T-shirt. On the front, there was a drawing of a bird in flight.

"That's nice," Blatzo said. "I don't see anything to get mad about."

Then he looked at the back of the shirt. In big letters it read *NUMBER ONE BIRD NERD*.

"Grrr," said Blatzo. "Time to run."

Nobody ran.

The little girl from kindergarten tugged on Blatzo's hand and made him kneel down so they were the same height.

She gave Blatzo a hug. "Bird Nerd, thanks for saving them!"

Blatzo turned red.

"Hang on," Justine said. "There's another present in the bag for you."

Blatzo stood and reached into the bag again. He pulled out some folded pieces of soft and colorful cloth that looked like diapers.

"Huh?" he said.

"Since you care so much about the environment, you can be the first in school to use them," Justine said. "I'm selling them now instead of plates made from pig pee."

"Pig urine," Blatzo corrected.

"Call it what you like, but I learned the hard way that people think of it as pig pee. And people just don't want to eat off plates made from recycled pig pee."

"So you're selling window wipes?" Blatzo asked. "Window wipes made from recycled material?"

"Do you have any idea how much toilet paper gets used every day?" Justine said. "People want soft toilet paper, which doesn't contain any recycled material. Soft toilet paper is really, really bad for the environment. So we need to get people to use those instead."

Blatzo dropped the cloths back into the bag like they were poisonous snakes.

"Don't worry," Justine said. "Nobody has used those ones. Yet."

"Yet?" Blatzo asked.

51

"You'll love them," Justine said. "They're softer than toilet paper. And after you use them, you throw them in a wet bag until the end of the week. Then simply wash all of them and reuse!"

"Great flagpole story," Michael said after a short silence. "But I still have to vote false."

"False," Safdar said. "Definitely false. Reusable toilet wipes?"

"I'm with them," Blatzo said. "You'd have to be crazy to believe in something like reusable toilet wipes."

Justine glared at Michael, Safdar and Blatzo. "That wasn't a flagpole story. And it's true. I have order forms and everything."

"Oops," Blatzo said.

"So," Justine asked them. "Do any of you want to help me start selling them door to door after school today?"

"Can't believe how late it is," Blatzo said, looking at his watch. "Time to run."

And they did. Michael and Safdar and Blatzo. They ran like scared little kids.

JUSTINE McKEEN
and the BIRD NERD

Notes for Students and Teachers

Birds of all kinds are so beautiful that this is reason enough to want to help protect them. But birds are also very important to the environment, so it's crucial for us to take the steps we can to reduce the number of deaths from man-made hazards, especially collisions with windows.

Some green projects are so big and challenging that we need to work across many levels of society to make a difference. However, student and school projects that work within the community can help our feathered friends improve their chances of survival.

Chapter One

Yes, there really are plates made from pig urine, for all the reasons that Justine uses in her sales pitch.

Time Magazine included it in the article, "Top 10 Odd Environmental Ideas." *www.ti.me/TJob1c*

Chapter Four

If you find an injured bird, Jimmy Blatzo's advice will help you care for it. If you want to know more, here's a handy website address:
www.toronto.ca/lightsout/injured.htm

Chapter Eight

As reported by *Audubon magazine*, Jimmy Blatzo's report to council members gives a sad but accurate picture of the dangers that windows present to birds.
http://mag.audubon.org/articles/birds/when-birds-and-glass-collide

Chapter Nine

Putting decals up on your school and home windows will really help birds avoid collisions with glass. The web has many different resources to help you

create your own decals. One great site is here:
http://flap.org/residential.php

Chapter Ten

A few years ago, *The New York Times* reported that forests are being *wiped* out to make toilet paper. (That pun was no accident!) The solution that Justine hopes more people will try is, of course, reusable toilet wipes.

www.livescience.com/7688-extreme-green-reusable-toilet-wipes.html

Sigmund Brouwer is the bestselling author of many books for children and young adults. *Justine McKeen and the Bird Nerd* is the fifth title in his series about Justine and her efforts to create a greener community. Sigmund loves visiting schools and talking with youth of all ages about reading and writing. To learn how to invite Sigmund to your school, please visit *www.rockandroll-literacy.com.* To download free ebooks from the author — great for the environment!— go to *www.myrockandrollbooks.com.*